WINGMAN

A BLACK SEQUINNED BOWS AND CHAMPAGNE NIGHTS PREQUEL

NOVELLA

JUDE E. McNAMARA

TWO JUDES PUBLISHING

CONTENTS

CHAPTER 1

~"If You Didn't Get Dirty, You Didn't Play"~

Love and loyalty are powerful forces. Loyalty compelled my need to get into the game. Love beckoned me on a path to catch the curve ball headed my way. Truth is, when a curve ball is making a beeline your way, you have no clue as to where it might land. Unlike the fastball, a curve ball can be wildly unpredictable. You only have a few brief moments to adjust. A mere split of a second to adapt to changing conditions.

Me, I was accustomed to fastballs. In the game of life and love, I am the fastball king. I have spent my entire young adult existence living my life in the fast lane. Take your pick. Fast food. Fast planes. Fast cars. Even fast women. I've mastered them all.

Particularly fast women.

Hell, I even lost my head and married one. She's definitely soon to be the ex Mrs. Noah Dunham. What I need now more than anything is a fast divorce. My heart and mind relish the day I can extract this gold ring from my finger. It feels like a golden noose rather than the symbolic infinity knot calling me to love, honor, and obey.

In hindsight, my decision to marry was a moment in my life when I exercised poor judgment. I had failed to heed the advice of my best friend Lucas Cook. If only I could turn back the hands of time. The last eighteen months I have been living in a hellhole called my marriage.

Lucas and I met six years ago at the United States Naval Academy—both of us presidential appointees to the Academy. Both of us came from well-to-do families with fathers who were career military. As dormitory roommates, we immediately hit it off. It was here we learned the importance of having responsibility for each other.

We grew to become best friends who cherished the benefits of having each other's backs. Loyalty is a necessary element to the art of surviving military college. Consequently, Lucas and I kept each other's confidences. We shared our past mistakes. We shared our future dreams. We boasted to anyone that got in our way that we were 'brothers from another mother.' If you messed with one of us, you messed with both of us.

We studied together. We protected each other. We relied on each other. It was second nature to respect each other's advice.

Except for the one time I lost my mind in a mound of hot pussy, failing to heed his words. Words that looked and sounded like "don't marry her."

A fine brown ass in the palm of my hands coupled with beautiful thick lips wrapped around my cock had momentarily seized my wits. She was a potent drug that had scrambled my brain in ways I couldn't explain even to myself. I should have heeded Lucas's advice to "just say no." But my lust meter for her had ridden off the charts. In the words of Tina Turner, "What's love got to do with it?" Absolutely nothing. Lust prevailed over love. And now I have spent the last eighteen months fucked twenty ways to Sunday, stuck in a marriage with a woman I can't stand.

Now I'm riding the rails of divorce. I can't get off the marriage train fast enough. Regrettably, she is the fastball I had no business taking a swing at. But that's another story for another day. Which brings me back to the matter of curveballs.

You see, the game of life is filled with many curveballs. Curveballs require you to adjust. They require you to adapt. They require you to move fast. They require you to change. There aren't a lot of choices with curveballs. Your options are typically limited to a single choice. And once you see it coming—*WHAM.* You have to decide.

Today is the beginning of a journey wherein I would be faced with one of life's curveballs. I didn't give it a second thought, even knowing how unequipped and unprepared I was for the moment. There were no other logical choices. So I made the decision to swing. It didn't matter because I was swinging in the name of love. I was swinging in the name of loyalty. I was swinging in the name of brotherhood.

Love. Loyalty. Brotherhood. A combination that made for a powerful curveball.

Lucas was the pitcher. I was the catcher. She was the batter.

The curveball coming my way had a name.

Riley Nelson.

CHAPTER 2

~"As the Season Goes On, Teammates Go From Teammates to Friends, to Brothers"~

Lucas and I were the only two lieutenant commanders in the officer's box this year. Both of us towered in the corner, him being six feet tall, and myself two inches taller. All the other officers were of a higher rank, and the fact that I was the only African American lieutenant commander in the box made the moment all the more a command performance for me.

We were at the annual Army-Navy game at Lincoln Financial Field. The Army-Navy game, steeped in tradition, marked the end of the regular college football season. It was also the third and final game of the season's Commander-in-Chief Trophy series. It was a long-standing tradition that Lucas and I attended whenever we were lucky enough to be stateside. We each had a standing invitation to today's game. We were anointed the next generation of the Navy's senior officers who were being fast-tracked for the admiral ranks. Both of us expected to make captain in a few years.

Fast track. There it is again. Back to fast. The single thing that had turned my life upside down these last eighteen months. Life in the fucking fast lane.

"I begged you not to marry her, man. I specifically said 'only date her,' Noah.' I did not say go the hell off and fucking marry the woman."

"As far as I'm concerned Lucas, you're to blame. You introduced us. I'm not going to cry over spilled milk. I simply want out.

"Don't think for one minute you're going to lay this at my feet. Oh hell, no. You only have yourself to blame for not listening to me." Lucas was shaking his head, looking half-amused, half like he might be about to punch me.

I was hardly surprised. Lucas was not going to let me off the hook or let me shift the blame. He was right. I did this to myself. And now I was paying for my own mistake.

"You and I've been arguing my mistake for a year. Give up the ghost, dude. I fucked up. Can you please stop rubbing salt in the wound?" I spread my hands wide in surrender.

This was our regular routine whenever we got together. I bitched about my marriage; he blamed me for not taking his advice. I expressed my deep regrets; he reminded me to have hope in better days ahead. Rinse and repeat.

I knew my failed marriage was causing Lucas some level of emotional pain. He hated watching me be so miserable. He had no roadmap for how to handle my personal setback. He was used to me being the one to dole out sound advice. I was typically the life of the party. And these days even I knew I was no fun.

"Thank God we won't be arguing over this five years from now. I can't keep locking you up in my home every week filling your glass with Stoli, talking you down off the ledge. You owe me this time, Noah. If it weren't for me, those JAG Corp boys might have you in their clutches by now for killing your wife," Lucas laughed, breaking the tension.

I knew he was joking. Neither of us were violent men. We rescued women. We didn't harm them. We were Navy pilots. We were also black belts. Which meant we could be mean blue killing machines when faced head-on against the enemy. The Navy had invested well over a million dollars in our training. We were stellar in the air and your worst nightmare on the ground. Alpha dogs. With women, we liked to think of ourselves as love machines. But you couldn't tell it by my behavior these days. The last several months I had leaned hard on Lucas just to get through my days. There was nothing about me that resembled a love machine.

"I'm a naval officer. I hate dirty. I need precision. I had to hire a housekeeper so I can live in my own damn house. Casey's a couch potato on steroids. All she does is watch reality television or soap operas all day. Oh yeah, except for when she takes time out for fucking."

"Which is exactly why I said the words out loud and clear. Date, yes. Marry, no. What part of the memo did you not get? Do I look like the jackass whisperer to you, Noah?"

I glanced down on the football field taking note of the quarterback sneak that was in play. I shrugged my shoulders, temporarily feigning ignorance and looked up to the ceiling as if to be pondering the ways of the world in deep thought, my index finger placed on the side of my cheek. "Yup. You do."

Lucas looked at me with frustration. He closed his eyes, shaking his head. I tried not to laugh, but I couldn't help myself. Hell I very much felt like a certified jackass. The shoe fit, so I was gonna wear it.

We both started laughing, Lucas raising his hand to give me a high five. That was how we rolled. We made light of bad situations. Lucas was laughing, his attempt at trying to cheer me up. And I was laughing to keep from crying.

The good news was my divorce was practically imminent. My future as a free man was the single thing I relished most. That, and my friendship with Lucas. It was because of him that I was able to put one foot in front of the other each day. He gave me stability, confidence and a reason to wake each morning. Lucas, the eternal optimist, reminded me often of that old cliché that 'misery does not last always.'

"Can you believe we're losing this game?" he sighed, glancing through the glass box window, his eyes fixed on the scoreboard. Navy was down two touchdowns.

I peered out the window overlooking the stadium filled with thousands of fans. It looked like a sea of blue, white, gold, and green. Half the uniformed fans were men and women dressed in Navy whites. The other half were dressed in Army green. You could sense the electric energy emanating off the field was being felt by the fans in the stands. A pang of nostalgia swept over me. The atmosphere was much more lively with the college kids in the stands than up here in this glass sardine can otherwise known as the officer and gentlemen box. Those were the good old days.

"Fucking Army," Lucas grunted. "We're behind fourteen points."

"It's only the first half, Lucas. Chill, man. We'll pull out a win before it's over. Keep the faith."

"I don't know Mico. Are you paying attention? Army's quarterback is on fire. He's firing that sheepskin like it's a missile."

The fact that Lucas had called me by my academy nickname "Mico" only reminded me how much we operated like family. Besides Lucas, only a handful of folks—mostly my family—called me Mico. It was a nickname given to me by grandmother. I was christened Noah Michael Dunham. My grandfather was also named Noah, so Grandma called me Mico for short. It was her way of distinguishing me from her husband, but not many people were privy to that little fun fact besides me.

"You stress too much, Lucas. Need I remind you that for the last six years Navy has won?"

"Yeah, well all things change Mico."

"Don't jinx this game, dude," I said casually, both of us half-bored with the game. We were losing. Lucas and I were winners. Neither of us handled losing well. Not in sports. Not in life.

*****

My eyes tracked the cute blond server headed our way with a tray filled with chilled vodka martinis. *The officer's box does have its perks.* Vodka and beauty combined together. Just in time. A welcome addition to this room full of crotchety old naval brass.

Being able to rest my eyes on pretty was a sweet change of pace from these old-timers sucking up the oxygen in the room, regurgitating stories about missions of long ago.

My eyes raked over the pretty blonde again. She was wearing a crisp white shirt unbuttoned down to the crevice of her boobs. Her black pencil skirt hugged her ass so tight I had an urge to show her what real lead feels like. It took everything I had not to whip out my old playa card and back that ass up into the nearest storage closet.

Lucas grabbed two more vodka martinis off blond Barbie's round tray. He handed one of them to me, giving her a wink all in the same pass. He raised his eyebrows at me, reading my dirty mind. I stretched my spine, my six-foot-two frame towering over Blondie.

She blinked her eyelashes, her red lips pressing together, smiling politely at Lucas. She turned her head my direction, her eyes sweeping down to my crotch, then back up again, giving me a second once over. A warm smile spread across her face. A look that got my adrenaline pumping.

"Thank you. My friend here needs this drink to get through this game," Lucas grinned.

"That's what I'm here for, Commander. You know, to help you enjoy the game."

Lucas flashed his million-dollar smile at her. That sounded like a double entendre to me.

"Really now?" I spoke, her forwardness catching me off guard. "How sweet is this?"

She blushed, her face turning a bright red. She looked as if she hardly knew whether to engage with Lucas first or me. Her mouth parted, but no words came out. She turned her head towards me. I slid my left hand bearing my ring finger into my pocket.

"He's married," Lucas grinned, noticing my sloppy attempt at hiding my marital status.

He slapped me on my back, a display of brotherly camaraderie.

No doubt, as soon as my divorce is final, I was going to reactivate my playa card for however long it took for me to forget Casey's name. Lucas wouldn't get this chance to cock block me in the future. Though I was happy to know I hadn't lost all my skill at catching a pretty woman, I still considered myself a man of honor who wouldn't touch one until his divorce was final. I would sure as hell work the eyeballs, though. I wasn't dead yet.

The waitress turned her attention back to Lucas, waiting for a signal. He ran his fingers through his blond hair, his eyes wandering across her body. I knew that move. That was Lucas's tell. He was contemplating his next move. I could practically hear the wheels in his brain turning.

"So is he," I added with a straight face. "Married." I decided I'd blow his game up too. Turnaround cock blocking was fair play wasn't it?

Blondie huffed, darting away from the both of us at lightening speed.

"What kind of fucking wingman are you exactly?" Lucas groaned. "Dude, you know I'm not married. I don't even have a girlfriend. What the fuck, Mico?"

"Misery loves company, brother. One for all and all for one, wingman."

"I should have flashed my tattoo at her. Then made you show her yours," I teased back at him while taking a huge swig of my vodka.

"God, no. Then she might have wanted to take us both on at one time," Lucas said. "Brothers in arms. Get it?"

"You actually said that with a straight face, motherfucker," I chuckled.

My mind drifted back to the time Lucas and I were on leave together. We had gone on a bender. The bender lasted several days, and ended in matching tattoos, which were a nod to a ritual we had created for ourselves. Whenever we flew on squadron drills or crucial missions, our ritual was to bump fists. I would shout "Rock-out, Wingman!" and Lucas would answer

17

back "Rock-in, Wingman." It was our way of wishing the other safe travels. Our good luck mantra. At the end of this particular bender, Lucas and I had our mantra branded on our upper arms as a permanent reminder of our brotherhood.

"Thank God your wife didn't extinguish all the dog in you. I was beginning to believe she'd cut your balls off, too."

"I'm not a dog, Lucas."

"No?"

"No. I paused for effect. Then I answered, "I'm a wolf in sheep's clothing."

We both laughed so loud, we turned a few curious heads in the room.

"You know, Mico, I never wanted her for your wife. You were only supposed to hit it and quit it."

"Well I hit it. Now we're quitting it."

"Thank God."

"I know, right?"

"Don't mind me for giving you a hard time, Mico. I only want you to be happy. No one knows better than me that you're not one to walk away from challenges."

A moment of silence passed between us. Lucas took another big swig of the chilled vodka, this time sliding an olive-filled toothpick between his lips. He wiped the corner of his lip with the edge of the blue and gold cocktail napkin, his sharp blue eyes meeting mine. A grin suddenly stretched wildly across his face, his hand sweeping his blond hair across his brow.

"God bless the quitters, man."

I grinned back at him. "Man, you are so full of shit." I raised my hand to high five him. We clinked our glasses.

CHAPTER 3

~"Nod Your Head and Give the Signal to the Pitcher"~

I surveyed the buffet table filled with food. I was getting hungry. Part of me appreciated this prestigious box, but another part could not make peace with the buffet-style table filled with food that had no business being eaten by any military man with a brain. Did caviar, scallops, crab legs and pasta count as real food at a football game? I think not. This extravagant buffet was a crime against football.

I scanned the box again. Many of the room attendees, namely the admiral, his wife, and his cronies were starting to get wasted. Their voices were louder now. An aura of gaiety had begun to fill the room.

The admiral and his crones yelled noisily as Navy intercepted the ball, the receiver running straight for the goal line. Lucas and I both sat on the edge our seats, yelling, "go" out loud like every other member of the brass in the box.

"What did I tell you Lucas? Navy's going to win."

"Yeah well it ain't over until the fat lady sings."

"You know what we need, Lucas?"

"Exactly," he said, reading my mind before I could finish my sentence.

"Hot dogs," I said.

"Beer," he answered.

"After you."

Lucas and I made our way out of the officers' box, notably minding our manners, making sure we made small chit chat with the brass as we headed for the double doors leading to the concrete concourse. The smell of real food was only a few long strides away.

A trio of pretty girls giggling loudly were walking past us in the opposite direction, up the concourse towards the brass box-seat section we'd just left. Lucas turned around to follow them having lost sight of our beer and hot dog mission, his sense of direction compromised by hot sexy booty walking the opposite way. I grabbed his arm tightly, spinning him back around towards the aroma of the hot dogs. The girls giggled even louder. The noisy cheers from the fans in the stands sounded much closer now that we were blending in with the mainstream fans.

"Jailbait, Lucas. Focus"

"Damnnnnn. I want to scoop all three of them up at one time. The three of us can get to know each other six different ways. Good God, Mico. What has the world come to, brother? We've been out to sea too long."

"You know you're getting too old for these pretty young things. They're probably the daughters of a few of these Army generals. Or better yet, the admiral's kids. Trust me. I'm saving you from yourself."

"I've got no problem trying to tap that long enough to find out," Lucas said, his eyeballs still not back in his head.

"You might tap the wrong ass and get forced into a marriage you can't get out of, brother."

"I'm okay with that Mico. Military brats make great wives. They come ready made for the military life. That's the kind of wife you should be looking for next time around."

I waited for his brain to catch up to the fact I called him old. He hates it when I do that, but I owe him one for driving the nail in my coffin over Casey.

Wait for it.

"Besides, since when did this side of thirty make me old?"

And there it was.

"Since those gals are barely breaking twenty that's when. And for the record, there will be no next time around for me, man. I've paid my dues to the gods of marital bliss. They can have that shit. It's all about me now, Lucas."

"Nah, man. Your feathers are just singed, Mico. You need to get your wings back so you can fly like the eagle we know you are. Time will heal your heart." Lucas nudged his elbow in the side of my ribs.

"My heart was never in it. It was my dick that got caught in Casey's vice. Once this divorce is over, I'm sending my dick to the school of the big head. He ain't surfacing again, until he learns to behave. I'm turning my dick into a fucking commander."

"You're trippin' Mico. You know Casey turned you out."

"Fuck you man."

We both laughed, weaving in and out of the thick crowd of fans, most of whom had the same idea as us. It was half time. Everybody in this place wanted the same thing we wanted. Food. Beer.

*****

Lucas and I strolled towards the concession counter, having grabbed a couple of cold beers on the way down the concourse. We were waiting our turn in line to order, debating the merits of hot dogs versus Philly cheese steaks.

Just as we moved up in the line, before either of us knew what was happening, a beautiful goddess slipped in a puddle of spilled soda. She tripped in front of us wearing a pair of fuck-me-right-now-this-minute heels, one of which had broken underneath her. She fell forward, bumping into Lucas on the way down, chilidogs splattering across the front of his Navy dress whites. Her short denim skirt slid high above her caramel-colored thighs, revealing skimpy lace camouflage-print panties with *Army* written across the butt in pink lettering. Oh my. Victoria does indeed keep secrets. Ab-so-fucking-lutely-perfect.

"Oh my God," she squealed, a blush spreading across her face, her big brown almond eyes looking upward, pinning Lucas in place.

Lucas reached down towards the cold wet concrete, lifting her up in his arms, looking as if he'd been hit by a meteor. An expression of wonder etched across his face, followed by one of heated desire.

I whispered to him under my breath. "Man, the stars and heaven are opening up for you now. Don't mess this up. Do. Not. Let. Her. Get. Away."

This chick brought real meaning to the words 'drop dead gorgeous.' Exotic. Nice toned legs. Big brown eyes. Long brown hair with a wispy bang that blew across her forehead with the gust of breeze around us. She had that girl-next-door look. An angel sent from heaven with a French fry hanging off the side of her long brown curls.

Lucas had lost his ability to speak. He was staring at her as if he didn't know his own goddamned name. She was all he could see. I punched him in the side, hoping that would force him to speak his own damn name out of his mouth.

"Are you okay? Can I get you anything? More chilidogs maybe?"

Finally he speaks.

Lucas was still holding her in his arms as if he were afraid she might get away. Hell, I would have held on to her too. She looked anxious. Gorgeous, but anxious. Ready to take flight any second.

"God, I'm so embarrassed. I'm so sorry," she muttered, breathing heavily. "I was rushing to get back to my seat. My brother Reese, he's quarterbacking for Army. I didn't want to miss him. Oh my God, I'm so sorry—"

Army? My boy Lucas is dancing with the devil now. *My mind fast-forwarded to the notion of naval officer and army brat. How does that work exactly?* If only he would snap out of this daze. I'd never seen him like this. Star struck. Lost for words. This was a first.

25

The goddess moved to grab napkins out of what was left of her chaotic food tray, which she was still holding with one hand. She nervously began wiping his shirt, smearing chili sauce across his already stained shirt.

Lucas looked a hot mess. God, I wished I had a camera. I clinched my jaw to keep from laughing. He was oblivious to the mess she was making across his chest because his stare was completely focused on her face. She blushed as her tongue swiped her pretty pink fuckable lips. Lucas still hadn't let go of her. She kept babbling endlessly about how sorry she was until finally more words rolled out of Lucas's mouth.

"I'm Lucas. Lucas Cook. I'm fine. Really."

"Riley. Riley Nelson," she said shyly, her rich brown eyes peeking through her lashes as she glanced up at him. She reached her index finger up to his face to wipe at a blob of chili sauce that had splattered across his check. Then she stuck her chili-dipped finger in her mouth, licking it clean.

Boom. The crown jewel. Curveball. Cupid's arrows mainlining straight to Lucas's heart.

I watched them at distance, but I was close enough to hear Lucas mumble something to her in Italian, his Italian-American roots taking over his brain. I knew where this was going next. Tender whispers in Italian were

Lucas's signature move. *Now we're talking. That's right buddy. Get in there. Get in the game. Seal the deal.*

Whoa. Italian words were passing between them. Did she just answer back in Italian? I'll be damned. She had. Goddess was rising to the occasion, catching Lucas off guard. Riley Nelson was knocking Lucas off his game. *She smacked that one straight out of the park.*

I was on the sidelines looking in on this scene but I was as stunned as he was. I had no idea what words were passing between them, but whatever was being said, it surely sealed the deal. These two never let go of each other.

*****

I stood at the top of the concourse as Lucas walked Riley back to her seat, helping her carry a fresh tray of chilidogs while limping on a broken heel. It was cute to watch her painfully embarrassed as she approached her family, a tall naval officer on her heels, his head held high with chili smeared across his shirt. I watched them from a distance, exchanging polite pleasantries.

I would later learn from Lucas that Riley's father was a lieutenant colonel in the Army, stationed at Aberdeen Proving Ground. Riley was biracial, her mother was French Canadian, which explained her exotic-looking appeal. She and her brother Reese had grown up as military brats traveling around the world to wherever her father's career led. Thus she was fluent in several languages.

It would seem marriage hadn't only found me. Lucas had found his match. His military brat. He was a goner from the day she fell at his feet.

While Navy had lost the game that day thanks to Riley's brother Reese, the day was a win for Lucas. Because two years later, wedding bells were ringing. Lucas and Riley married in the small chapel in Annapolis. And me, I was divorced.

It would be many years before I would ever see Riley Nelson Cook again after that day. His was not the only heart she would capture.

CHAPTER 4

~"Behind Every Great Pitcher There is a Great Catcher"~

While time and distance had Lucas and me on different continents, it hadn't made our bond of friendship any less close. Ten years later, Lucas and I remained the best of friends. In fact, we were closer. We were both on our second tour of duty.

Changing technology allowed us the freedom of to stay in touch during our deployments. We met often whenever we could, depending on what part of the world we were occupying. We stayed in touch despite the separation of miles between us.

For years, I had been on a highly classified mission for the Secretary of Defense, a project that had kept my wings on the ground more often than I cared to be this second tour. Lucas had been stationed in Malaysia while I had been globetrotting all over the world.

I hadn't remarried. I'd been single almost a decade, busy sowing my oats across the globe. There never seemed to be the right time or the right woman to make me want to throw a stake down, plant roots and marry again. While I had plenty of women friends to occupy my time, none of them made my world turn on its axis. It didn't matter, though I found myself to be homesick much of the time.

I lived outside of D. C., but I was never home long enough to enjoy all that it had to offer. Being away from home so much would have been a ton harder had it not been for my friendship with Lucas. As always, he kept me grounded.

I was bummed I had missed his wedding eight years ago, unable to stand up as his best man. I was grumpy for a few weeks over having missed his vows, but my mission left me no other option. I had also missed the birth of Lucas and Riley's two kids, but Lucas kept me in the loop. He made sure I had all the baby pictures, little league pictures, and dance recital videos. I even had pictures of Riley in various stages of both pregnancies. Lucas was a lucky man.

I had the occasional hello and good-bye by telephone a couple of times with Riley. Whenever I called, Lucas insisted she say hello, then excitedly grabbed the phone away to catch up with me. As a result, she and I never really engaged in meaningful conversation. While I didn't know Riley well, I felt like I did. And I knew how much Lucas loved her. She was all he ever talked about. He wanted me to know everything about her.

It seemed I grew to love her as much as he. It pleased me that she made him happy. He was as much in love with her a decade later as he was the day he met her. And I could see why. She was beautiful. A great wife. A wonderful mother. Through the years she had even started to build her own food and wine business. She was creative. She had a pretty good head for business, too. With everything Lucas shared about Riley, what was there not to love? I loved Lucas. And I loved his family as if they were my own.

Lucas and I spoke in a few of our phone conversations about his family and me cruising the Mediterranean someday in the future. We fantasized about the day our careers would slow, allowing us to put our personal lives front and center. I used to tease him that we needed to speed up the plan. Time was getting away from both of us.

Lucas's son Xavier was eight. His daughter Samantha, six. The kids were growing like weeds. From the pictures and family videos Lucas sent, Riley had grown to be more beautiful every day. I never missed a chance to remind Lucas that we needed to get our shit together, move the game plan along or else the kids would be adults. Of course he shrugged me off, declaring that he was still well on this side of forty and that age was nothing but a number. I expected that to be a declaration he would continue to make for years to come. I chuckled whenever he insisted we weren't getting older. Nothing had changed.

Lucas and Riley had built a home in Washington Crossing, Pennsylvania, not far from Lucas's twin sister Zoe. He was looking toward the future when he made the decision to plant roots in Pennsylvania. He had grandiose plans for his retirement. He figured that with his connections in New York he could guest lecture at Columbia University, commuting from Washington's Crossing. The fact that his twin sister lived there made it convenient for his kids to have extended family nearby. I hadn't given much thought to how my life would unfold after retirement. Maybe I would meet "the one" too, and settle down. Perhaps I would live somewhere close to Lucas. He and I could kick back together, play golf on the weekends, watch some football, and throw back Stolis on the regular.

*****

Today was special for both of us. Both Lucas and I were stateside. Our schedules were intersecting. It didn't happen often, but this weekend it did. We considered it a treat to be in the same time zone together. We would make sure to take full advantage of it.

We were meeting in Philadelphia this afternoon. Lucas had phoned me yesterday to give me a heads up that he had a pressing problem of an urgent nature. Whatever was bothering him, he didn't want to discuss it over the phone.

I figured maybe the Navy was calling on him to do something or go somewhere he wasn't happy about. We often had assignments that made us bitch and growl, but we went forward with the assignments nonetheless. For our weekend starters, we were meeting for lunch at a restaurant inside the Rittenhouse Hotel off the square in Philadelphia. Lucas said the restaurant was owned by a renowned chef who was a friend of Riley's.

As I drove my Porsche into downtown Center City, I was starting to feel excited. Today would be a good day. Lucas and I would see each other again.

CHAPTER 5

~"A Friend is a Person Who Will Make a Great Scoop When You Happen to Throw One in the Dirt"~

"Welcome, Sir," the valet said as I pulled into the circular drive in front of the prestigious Rittenhouse Hotel. The young valet opened my door, his eyes widening at the shine bouncing off the sunlight as it hit my brand new white Porsche Carrera. I smiled.

"Take care of my baby," I said, as I tossed the key fob his direction.

"Not a problem sir," he said, his eyes widening as he stepped inside, running his hand across the dark wood paneled dashboard.

My love for fast cars hadn't changed through the years. I took great pleasure in putting my new wheels on I-95 today. I strolled inside the hotel, my excitement building at the thought of seeing Lucas again. It had been a little short of a year since we had seen each other last, and I was looking forward to seeing him in person. I wanted to take him for a spin in the new ride. I rode up the elevator pushing the bright red button for the second floor where the Lacroix restaurant was located.

"Noah, over here," Lucas called out, walking towards me down the long entryway lined with an etched-glass partition. Glimmering chandeliers were sparkling from above, the restaurant atmosphere inviting.

I took long strides toward Lucas, meeting him halfway, giving my best friend a huge bear hug. It was an emotional moment. Lucas and I had spoken on a regular basis, but being in the same space again was heartwarming. I had missed my friend.

"Man, you're looking well. You haven't aged a day since I saw you last," I laughed.

"That was only ten months ago, Mico. Lucas laughed, falling in sync with me.

"Well in that case, neither have you, buddy. I see you still holding down the six pack," Lucas teased, punching me in the stomach with both fists, his playful punches hitting my brick wall of muscle.

"You look good too, Lucas. Family life suits you."

"She takes good care of me," he said, swatting me on the back.

I noticed a hint of pain flash across his face that wasn't matching his words. Only someone that knew Lucas well would have seen it. I wondered if everything was okay.

I sensed something was wrong, but I would have to wait for him to share with me. Lucas was the type that generally had to wind himself up before sharing his pain. Much like a slow pitch. So I waited. I waited for the curveball that I suspected was coming.

"Riley's friend owns this restaurant. I hope you don't mind? We're at the Chef's table today. We'll have a front row seat to his culinary performance. Plus, we'll have a bit of privacy at the same time."

"Whatever you want man. It's your nickel."

A waiter dressed in black pants and a white shirt stood in the corner. A white Lacroix engraved towel was draped over his left arm. Seeing that we were ready, he walked our way, escorting us to a table that seated four. He welcomed us, pulling two of the place settings off the table. Lucas and I sat.

"Riley's friends with the chef. Chef Lacroix will be preparing our meal today. She says he's very good. I took the liberty of asking him to prepare a couple of porterhouse steaks for us. I hope that's okay?"

"Sounds good to me. Man, I'm hungry enough to eat the whole cow. The drive down from Virginia was tedious, lots of traffic. I didn't want to stop to eat, because I was so eager to get here. Porterhouse steak sounds perfect."

"Good. I ordered yours medium well."

"You remembered?"

"Of course. I wouldn't forget a fact as important as how a man eats his cow."

Sitting erect in my seat, I nodded in agreement. "I hear congratulations are in order, Commander Cook," I said casually.

"Thank you. Thank you," Lucas beamed. "I hear congratulations are in order for you as well, Commander Dunham. You're pinning it on next month right?

"That would be so, sir. At least I hear the paperwork is in play. You beat me to it by a few months, though. Not sure how I feel about being second this time."

"Get over it. Either way, it's awesome news. You beat me to the last promotion. Or did you forget, Mico?"

"How could I? We've been on this race to the top for what seems like the longest time. But I must say Lucas, commander suits you too, brother. You're wearing it well."

"I just ought to, Mico. I've got a couple of military brats to support. They're eating me out of house and home. This promotion came at a good time."

Lucas grinned his million-dollar smile, his ocean blues looking me over slowly, giving nothing away. But I knew something was gnawing at him.

The sommelier paused in front of us, interrupting. He was holding a black and gold leather-bound wine list, which he handed to Lucas. Lucas skimmed the list quickly, ordering a 1996 Louis Martini Amarone.

"What? No vodka martinis today? You getting soft on me, Lucas?

"My wife says we should drink this. Bear with me."

"You sound totally hen-pecked," I laughed.

Lucas grinned. We both knew it was true. The sommelier returned with the bottle, flashing the label under Lucas's nose. He nodded and the sommelier poured slightly more than a mouthful into Lucas's glass for him to taste.

Lucas swirled, sniffed, and then tasted, nodding his approval. We both waited in silence as the waiter filled our wine glasses before we began speaking again.

"Riley's becoming quite the wine connoisseur," I said, taking a swallow from my own glass.

"Yeah. I hardly know how she does it. She's been vigorously building her brand. She's raising our two kids. She's taking care of me. I don't know how she does it all."

Lucas wore an expression of amazement on his face.

"She is indeed a remarkable woman. Unlike me, you hit the jackpot Lucas when you got married," I nodded in agreement.

Lucas ignored my slight against Casey. We agreed years ago, after my divorce, not to bring up my ex-wife's name. Lucas was keeping to his word to our pact.

"Not to mention I had to add a kick-ass wine cellar addition to our home. I can't wait for you to see it, Mico."

"I can't wait to see it either."

I smiled back at him. This small talk was making me anxious. Whatever was bothering Lucas, I wanted him to come out with it.

"Yeah, and to top it off she wants another baby."

"Yeah, so make another one," I add casually, as the waiter arrives with two large plates of sizzling hot porterhouse steaks covered in Portobello mushrooms and small pearl onions. A dollop of chimichuri rests on the side of the plate against a pile of red potatoes and asparagus. It smelled delicious.

Lucas's fork with a bite of steak on the end stopped abruptly short of meeting his mouth at my last statement. He stared at me, his face blank.

"What? Motherfucker, you forget how to make a baby?" I asked. I was pretty sure I was looking at him as if he had two heads, perplexed as to why he suddenly stopped eating, acting as if he didn't understand English.

"Of course I know how to make a baby. It's not that, Mico," Lucas said with hesitation. "I've signed up for another tour of duty. Riley's not happy about it."

"Get the fuck out of here, dude. I signed up for another tour, too. I'm headed to Yemen."

"Yemen, Really? That's where I'm going. The USS Cole. We'll be on the same carrier, Mico."

"Well, rock the fuck out wingman," I answered with glee."

"Rock the fuck in wingman," Lucas answered back.

"This is best news I've had all day, Mico."

"We should celebrate. This will be like old times. We've talked about everything else these last few weeks. I can't believe this never came up."

"Me either Mico, but its all good now, my brother."

Lucas happily stuffed more steak in his mouth, chewing quickly. No doubt we were both ecstatic about this news. It was starting to feel like old times.

"Actually Mico, Riley's got her panties all in a bunch. She knows I'm leaving soon. She's not liking the fact I'm leaving again. She worries more these days about my not making it back home.

"What the fuck?" I ask, though this is a natural concern for military spouses. "Of course you'll make it back Lucas. Besides, I'm your wingman. No fucking way you won't make it back. Making it back home is what we do."

"Riley's got my head all fucked up. I need you to promise me that if anything happens to me on this tour, you'll take care of Riley and the kids for me. There's no one else I trust to watch over everything I hold dear. Riley, Xavier, and Samantha mean everything to me."

"Nothing is going to happen to you, Lucas. I'll be with you, dude. What's wrong with you? I won't let anything happen to you. I'll be damned if either of us will be coming home in a box."

I rest my fork for a minute. "What's with all this doom and gloom shit?"

This conversation was making me lose my appetite.

"Sometimes shit happens, Mico." Lucas looked as if he were in pain. Something was missing in this conversation. There had to be more pieces to what was starting to feel like a puzzle.

"Look, man. Stop tripping. We do the tour. We come back home. This ain't rocket science Lucas. You know how this works already."

"Right. You're right, Mico. I think I'm just all over the place. Riley's got me on the ledge. She and I are in the same book. We're just not on the same page right now."

"Pull yourself together Lucas," I ordered.

Lucas took a deep breath.

"I know you're playing it straight with me, Mico. I can't tell you how many times I wished you were closer by."

"I've missed you too. Keeping it real between us is what we do. Nothing is going to happen to you."

"Well if anything were to happen, promise me you'll watch over my family." He rubbed a hand across his jaw, his eyes searching mine.

Good Lord. It wasn't like Lucas to get paranoid because of another tour. This was was we did. We were career officers. Death could knock on the door any day of the week. We would just slam the door on the fucker's face. Lucas needed to get a grip.

"Look man, if it makes you feel better, I'll say the words out loud. I promise you on the Dunham name, on everything that I love, I will take responsibility for your family."

"Promise me, Noah."

Oh this was serious. He was back to calling me by my government name now.

"I promise you Lucas. If the tables were turned, I know you would do it for me. But I need for you to knock this shit off. You sound like a scared bitch. And we both know that is not who you are. You're not some minor-league rookie. We're major league. Commanders in the United States Navy."

"That's all I needed to hear."

"Uh huh. Good. Can we be done with this conversation now? Death and dying is bad for my digestion."

Lucas smiled his million-dollar smile. I was glad we were off this subject. But part of me felt like there were still more layers yet to be peeled. I went back to eating my steak.

*****

"Listen Mico. Changing the subject. There's something else I need to discuss."

Here it comes, I thought. *Now we were down to the real conversation.*

"Yeah, what?"

"You recall my time in Malaysia right?"

"Yup. Your last tour. What about it?"

I took a gulp of the Amarone. Umm. It was good. *Good choice Riley. I could get used to this.*

"You know sometimes shit happens man."

"Shit always happens. So what Lucas? What else is new?"

"This is hard for me, Mico."

We're back to Mico now. Now I'm gonna hear it.

"Get on with it, Lucas," I snapped.

I was starting to get irritated. I knew Lucas well enough to know that whatever he had to say, if he didn't come out with it soon I was going to take a crowbar to his ass and pry it out of him. This back and forth circling around the merry-go-round of what ifs was wearing thin on my patience.

"It's like this Mico—"

I listened intently to Lucas for the next fifteen minutes, taking in everything he had to say. He was spilling his guts. His words branding my heart, challenging the depth of my love for him. How far could we go? How far would we go?

When Lucas was done, I rested my fork yet again. I exhaled loudly, feeling as if he had knocked the wind out of me. I took a long deep breath. Then I took another big gulp of the fine wine Riley suggested we drink. I rose out of my chair and walked to Lucas's side of the table. Then I knocked him the fuck out of his chair with my fist. I watched him as he hit the floor. The waiter came running towards both of us at lightning speed as I stood over Lucas in disbelief.

Lucas rose halfway from the floor, raising his hand up at the waiter to shoo him off, holding his jaw with the other, his white napkin still hanging out from under his collar.

"It's okay," Lucas said to the waiter, waving him off, crawling up to his knees, then sitting back down. Lucas dropped his eyes to his plate, unable to look me square in the face. He swallowed the lump of food in his mouth, then took a large gulp of wine.

I could not believe my lying ears, and the waiter stood paralyzed, not sure what he should do next.
"This is what we do when we're having a meeting of the minds," Lucas said to the waiter who was rightfully nervous. "Bring more wine please."

"Bring a bottle of Jack," I huffed.

You would have thought we were a couple of mafia dons right then. Our shit looked weird, I know. I sat back down, working overtime to calm myself. I couldn't form words yet. I needed a minute to collect myself. The tension in the air was thick as we both sat in silence. Lucas made the first move to get us back on track, like he always did whenever we argued.

"Okay Mico. I deserved that. Did anybody ever tell you that you think with your fists first, your brain second?"

"Yeah motherfucker. You did."

"You can be a jackass sometimes."

"Yup. And that's why I keep you around. You're the jackass whisperer, remember?"

"That hurt you know," Lucas sighed, rubbing the side of his jaw, taking another swig of wine.

"My hand hurts more. Your jaw is made of rock."

We drank some more. And then we devised a plan. Our secret plan.

*****

For the next six years, Lucas and I were embedded in the war zone. We were stationed in the Persian Gulf heading up two squadrons in Yemen.

The advancements in technology were such Lucas that was able to Skype back home to Riley and the kids more often than not. We both cherished his connection to the family.

Our missions came with their own level of danger. Lucas had saved my life once while we were out on an assignment with the allied coalition. On one mission, I was almost shot down. Lucas was flanking me, taking the rebel forces out in the nick of time. A split second off, I might have been gone. Thankfully, we both made it back to the carrier safely. I was never so grateful as to have Lucas as my wingman. It was combat straight out of one of those Tom Cruise movies, except I was the best friend that came back alive. I was shaken emotionally once we both landed, grateful my friend had been there in the nick of time. But that was who we were. That was what we did. Brothers always taking care of each other. Lucas stepped down from his fighter jet, screaming like a wild man. He was yelling "Rock Out Wingman," as if he were some kind of crack-head on a high, happy as shit.

Once again, we had lived up to the meaning of our tattoos and were proud of it. Lucas had saved my life. He was beyond thrilled. And of course, I was even more thrilled to be alive. But beyond that, we both understood the gravity of that moment. Because once upon a time in Philadelphia, I too had saved his life.

47

Except the threat to his well-being was of a different nature. We were both indebted to each other. We didn't have to say any more words. The bond of love was there.

Lucas and I got to come home during the holidays that third tour. His family had grown. He had three kids now. Xavier was fourteen, Samantha was twelve, and baby Claire was three. Life was good for all of us. Lucas and I were still closer than brothers. Time and distance never changed that fact. But that third tour would be our last tour together. We never got to take that Mediterranean cruise.

CHAPTER 6

~ If You're Looking for the Ball, the Catcher Has It~

While the Navy had its own missions for Lucas and me, today I was on a mission of my own. A command performance. Years ago I kept confidences. Years ago I made promises. Eleven years is long past time for me to deliver on my word. A word that I gave in the name of love. A word that I gave in the name of loyalty. A word that I gave to my brother from another mother.

I stepped through the metal walkway boarding the American Airlines flight to Philadelphia. I pondered deeply the essence of this moment and what was to come ahead. I hoped Lucas would forgive me for my tardiness. I wondered whether Riley remembered me. Would she remember the day the stars aligned? The day when all providence moved? The day she met both Lucas Cook and me? A man whose life entwined with mine. With hers.

I had watched her now from a forced distance, keeping my silence. Eleven years. I trusted Lucas would forgive my timing. I had my reasons. Still, I'd been far enough away, yet close enough to act. It had been emotionally treacherous holding myself back all these years. She truly is irresistible. For I have loved her now almost as long as he did.

I've watched her grapple to build her own empire. Lucas would have been proud. She was a capable woman in so many ways. She was smart in the ways of business, yet naive to all manner of manipulative men. Men who would attempt to erase memories of Lucas from her heart. But Lucas was not erasable. I knew this because I too have loved him. Both of us loving her.

Now it was time for me to close the gap. I was keeping my word to honor and protect everything that Lucas held dear. Everything that I held dear.

I was coming for her. I was keeping my promise to Lucas. Except this time, I was not the catcher. I was not the pitcher. This time I was the hitter. And I was swinging for the fences. I was swinging in the name of loyalty. I was swinging in the name of brotherhood. I was swinging in the name of love.

Because when life throws you a curveball, you hit it out of the park.

~The End~

The follow-on story continues with Noah and Riley in the standalone novel **Black Sequinned Bows And Champagne Nights by Jude E. McNamara.**

This novel is available now at your favorite book retailer.

A Word About The Author

I am Jude E. McNamara. Virtual adventurer. Keyboard ninja. Guardian of sassy romantic encounters. I am the alter ego of that other woman, Jude. You know, the one that loves snowy nights, is in a relationship with love, and looking for her own hero. While by day she's off being the disciplined scrappy businesswoman with the mind of a shark, I gallivant her keyboard by night, running wild and free on the down-low. I figure she'll have to catch up to me. Because once that blue power button turns on, I'm far too busy breathing life into those colorful characters that run around in her head, incessantly telling me their stories even if it's at the break of dawn.

You can find me and my merry band of jet-setting girlfriends running from the paparazzi at the high-end cocktail bars in Manhattan, drinking Patron Silver. I'm the flashy one wearing the sparkly tiara on my head. Like clockwork, when she faithfully dons her track shoes to catch up with me, I usually have to listen to her lecture me about my behavior over a glass of champagne. She loves champagne. Actually I love champagne too—except I like mine with a side of tall, handsome hunk begging me to stop at the intersection of heartbreak hotel and romantic encounter road, demanding a happily ever after.

It's an arduous race to "The End" before her blue button goes dark and I cease to exist. But once the blue light appears, the race is on, right up to the point when we two Judes meet on the same page, often in a book like this one.

For more about the author, visit: www.judeemcnamara.com

Two Judes Publishing.

ACKNOWLEDGMENTS

A special thanks to my fabulous beta readers Donna Nelson, Jeanine Hillesland, Nicole Arnold, Kaerissa Nelms, Karol Lynn Fischer Davis, and Iris Kelly. Thank you for taking time to read this prequel and for providing me wonderful feedback and notes to deliver the best story possible. Your support has been invaluable. I'm a lucky gal to have you behind me in this writing journey. Thank again for reading this novella as well as my other novels.

To my readers around the globe, thank you for welcoming me into your world and for helping to make my dreams possible.

AUTHOR'S NOTE

Thank you for again for reading **WINGMAN.** The follow-on book ***Black Sequinned Bows And Champagne Nights*** continues with Noah and Riley's love story and is available at your favorite book retailer.

If you want to know more about Jude's new releases and sneak peeks, sign up here for her mailing list at www.judeemcnamara.com

Other Novels By Jude E. McNamara:

Black Sequinned Bows And Champagne Nights

Milk Money

Sugar Mommy On Top (upcoming release)

Stay Connected With Jude

www.judeemcnamara.com

Facebook, Twitter, Instagram, Pinterest